THE
SUNLIGHT
FAIRY

Also by Titania Hardie

FRANGIPANI FAIRIES: The Sunrise Fairy

And, coming soon...

FRANGIPANI FAIRIES: The Sunset Fairy

THE
SUNLIGHT FAIRY

Illustrated by Charlotte Middleton

SIMON AND SCHUSTER

First published in Great Britain in 2007
by Simon and Schuster UK Ltd, a CBS company.

Simon & Schuster UK Ltd
Africa House, 64-78 Kingsway, London WC2B 6AH.

A CIP catalogue record for this book is available from the
British Library.

ISBN 1416910832
EAN 9781416910831

1 3 5 7 9 10 8 6 4 2

Text design by Tracey Paris
Printed and bound in Great Britain.

www.simonsays.co.uk

For Zephy Losey and Maddie Kirby

Franni has
hidden some letters
within the pictures that
illustrate this story. They
make up the name of one of the
creatures she takes tea with. Can
you find all eight of them and
guess who it is?

She's jumbled the letters up
to make it a bit trickier,
but she's sure you'll be
able to work it out!
You can find the answer
on the Frangipani Fairies
website if you get stuck.

www.frangipanifairies.com

Chapter One

Just where the River Thames snakes around the bend between Hammersmith and Chiswick, on its way out of London towards Hampton Court Palace and Windsor Castle, is a row of old houses whose feet have been splashed by river-water every time there has been a high tide, for nearly two hundred years.

But the river coming in uninvited is a small price to pay when you can look up and downstream from morning to night from the windows in the living room! Sometimes, at dawn, these lovely old houses even seem magical, as the pale yellow sunshine plays across paintwork and filters through curtains.

Melissa Edwards is lucky enough to live in one of these houses. Her bedroom is in the attic, with a high sloping ceiling that casts interesting shadows. Her room faces the back

of the house and, though it isn't large, Melissa loves it. Her window nestles under the boughs of a beautiful old horse chestnut tree, and she likes gazing up at the green light that filters through its giant leaves.

Now, in late May, the tree is almost in full flower, and the scent of its blossoms comes in through her open window. But this afternoon, its wonderful smell is not quite enough to chase away Melissa's grey mood.

She is cross with her mother; and VERY, VERY cross with her baby brother. He has ruined her day.

On strict instructions from her mum, Melissa had been warned that her room had to be *sorted out properly* before she could go to Jemma's birthday party tomorrow.

"It's a tip in here, Melissa," Mum had said to her this morning. "I've scarcely been able to get through your door since your sleepover last weekend. I've been patient all week, but today's the day!

Your nail polishes must have almost dried out by now, there are hair products all over the floor, and I got body glitter between my fingers when I reached under your pillow for your nightdress this morning."

She paused, but Melissa knew her mum wasn't finished yet. "And those clothes in piles in the corner; how many wardrobe changes did you make? And don't think you can just stuff them back in your drawers or cupboard... Get the dirty ones into the laundry basket, and everything else neat and organised. Otherwise, you won't be going to that party tomorrow."

Melissa slumped down dejectedly on her bed. Everyone had had such a good time at the sleepover. It had been like a girls' spa weekend.

It was typical of Mum to only notice the mess and not to understand all the work that had gone into making it a success. Melissa hadn't really thought about the consequences: it had just been so much fun.

Emily had looked amazing with those long, false nails and eyelashes on, but now they were all stuck to Melissa's desk. She smiled at the memory of Jemma's hair after she and Sarah had finished plaiting it with ribbons and beads; the same ribbons which now lay discarded under her bed, while the beads were scattered across the floor, tangled in the long carpet. They'd take for ever to get out!

And what about those lipgloss kisses Chloe had left all over her mirror...

Melissa sighed deeply. It wouldn't be the same tidying up on her own, but she knew she had to start. Jemma's mum had hired a proper dance studio for the birthday party tomorrow, and Jemma's older brother was going to make a video of them all doing their

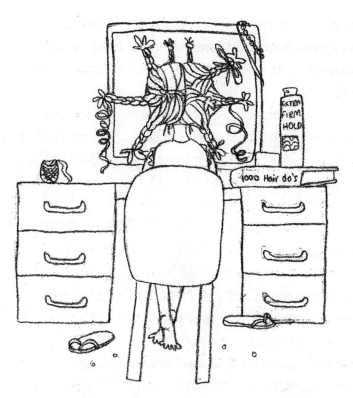

own routine to her favourite pop song. It was going to be so much fun! She *definitely* didn't want to miss that.

So Melissa worked hard for hours cleaning her room. She started by making her bed, which made a big difference, and this gave her the courage to take on the next challenge. The whole morning seemed to disappear while she cleaned, and tidied and put away her things.

She found toys she'd forgotten about, and tiny sweets all glued together in the strangest places!

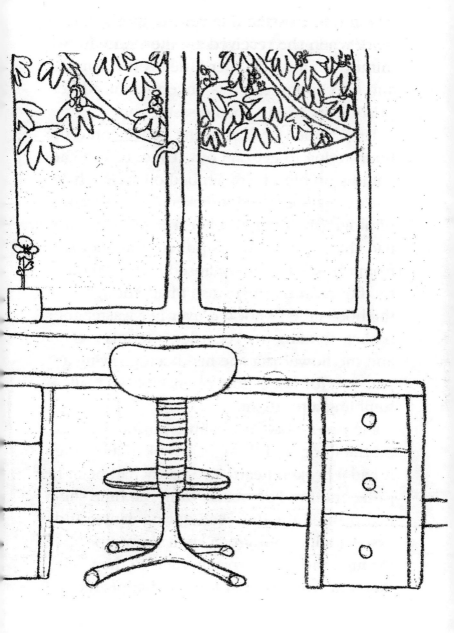

She was just standing back to admire her work when she received a visitor. And, in two minutes of mischief, her little brother Angus and his chubby, careless fingers, reduced her pristine space to a total disaster zone.

He'd tipped her colouring pencils onto the floor, trying to get one out. Then, before she could stop him, he'd climbed onto her chair *with dirty boots* and knocked down a framed photograph of her and her friends. The glass had shattered. As Angus pulled some books from the shelf, they collapsed in a heap on the floor. And, if that wasn't bad enough, the books then knocked over her wastepaper basket, sending her recorder, a tennis racket and the flower pot she had been growing a pansy in for her school science project, all tumbling after them.

Melissa looked at the little flower slumped on the floor, and thought it looked as though it had a broken heart! The pansy had been her pride and joy. For weeks, from the time she had planted the tiny seed during winter and first seen its stout green stem shoot up through the soil in spring, right to the moment when its first little bud appeared a fortnight ago, she had talked to it and laughed with it. Its face had three lovely colours – mauve, lemon-yellow and white; and it had a wonderful button-shaped eye that made her feel as though it could see exactly what she was thinking.

Now Melissa stood open-mouthed, staring at the chaos. Squealing with delight, colouring pencil finally in hand, Angus scuttled off, treading soil into her pale pink carpet as he left. The little pansy must have shuddered as it narrowly escaped his stomping feet.

Melissa was furious. She had wanted her room to be especially perfect to prove a point to her mum, and now she'd have to start all over again. She shouted and chased after her brother, then saw she was making an even worse mess with the flower on the carpet, so she flopped down and tried very hard not to cry.

Poor Melissa! She was a clever girl, and well organised most of the time. She liked to do her homework neatly, to keep her drawers in order, to fold her clothes away properly (except after sleepovers!), and to have flowers all around her. She had a good heart, too,

and was quite kind to
everyone, but if things
didn't go her way, she could get
very grumpy...

While Melissa was rubbing her eyes
and sniffing in the corner under the roof
beam, her little pansy, wrenched from its
comfortable spot on the window
sill, lay limply on the floor
in great distress. Its small
yellow eye took in the
scene of chaos stretching
across the little girl's
floor, and seeing her

looking so miserable with her arms clasped around her knees on the floor, it let out a sigh that perhaps no one could hear...

Chapter Two

$\mathcal{B}$ ut someone *did* hear it. Just a mile or so away along the river, in the Palm House at Kew Gardens, three pairs of eyes brightened.

Resting on the sun-drenched branch of a beautiful plumeria tree, which they used as a favourite terrace, three tiny fairy sisters were suddenly alerted to the sound of a text message arriving on their fairy-phone.

Putting aside her honey-dew cocktail, which she had been sipping from a bluebell flower, Leya, the eldest sister, leapt energetically to her feet. She was dressed in a hot pink

crop-top and matching frangipani-petalled skirt – perhaps rather shorter than her sisters' dresses – and she performed a quick handspring on the way to the fairy-phone without even appearing to notice she had done it. She printed the text message out onto a leaf and popped her favourite pink glasses on her nose. She read the message quickly and with great interest. "Ah-ha!" she said, as she crossed the sunny branch and handed the printed leaf to one of her sisters. "Distress call, Franni. This looks like a job for you. A little pansy tells me that her owner Melissa is having a total sense-of-humour failure. Her brother has driven her right over the edge."

The third and youngest sister, dressed in a vivid red dress, had hitched up her skirts and was cooling her feet in a water-filled shell. "But that little boy is always testing her patience, Leya. Is it worse than usual this time?" she asked with concern.

"Yes, Plum," Leya answered. "She's about to lose her cool with her mother, and her beautiful pansy flower needs rescuing. It's the little bloom she's been raising for a school project. She's spent a lot of time really nurturing that flower and was becoming quite a good little garden fairy herself, but I'm afraid she seems to have collapsed into a rather distressed state today. Her pansy is gasping for soil and water, and Melissa is too upset to notice!" She cart-wheeled over to a knot in the smooth tree-bark, and tickled it gently. A little screen appeared, and the fairy typed Melissa's name into a tiny keypad below it. A red dot immediately lit up and showed her the exact location of the girl and her sad little pansy.

Leya turned to her middle sister, who was busy reading the message inscribed on the leaf for herself. "This is a huge challenge, Franni – do you think you can help her to laugh again, and remind her that her little flower is dependent on her for help? There's no time to waste!"

Franni threw back a head of long, corn-yellow corkscrew curls and turned around, her face wreathed in smiles.

Her dress was made of beautiful white velvet
petals, tinged sun-yellow at the hem-line. Her
energy and character were just like the first
rays of sunshine in the morning, which make
you feel impatient to be out of bed, starting
your day and having fun.

She carefully set down the ladybird with whom she had been taking tea. Then, as a breeze entered the Palm House through an open window and whispered through the leaves, she gathered up her full white skirt. The pollen-coloured edges of the dress rustled softly on the branch as she sprang away.

"Don't worry, Leya! I know exactly where Melissa's house is. I'm on my way!" she called; and vanished, with only the sound of her laughter floating back on the warm, fragrant breeze.

Chapter Three

Melissa's nose was now getting blocked, and her cheeks were blotchy with tears. Her mother had heard the commotion, and arrived from the sitting room, two floors below. Angus was bellowing, and Melissa was feeling sorry for herself.

"Tears won't clear up this mess," her mother suggested quietly. It sounded to Melissa like her mum was protecting Angus, and letting him get away with it.

"But I've spent ages on my room, and look what he's done," she pleaded. "You never tell him off for coming in here and wrecking my things. That sign on my door says PLEASE KNOCK BEFORE ENTERING. But you always take *his* side!" Melissa sobbed.

Her mother laughed softly, but not without sympathy. "I think all mums try hard not to take anyone's side, you know," she said, trying to reason with her daughter, but Melissa didn't want to hear it. "I can't be everywhere all the time, Lissy. You're eight and Angus is only little. He didn't mean to do this." Mum looked sadly at the chaos.

Melissa knew this was true, but she couldn't give up her stubborn frown. Mum tried to make her smile a little. "Can't you see the funny side?"

Melissa couldn't. It was typical of her little brother to get round her mum all the time with a hug and a smile and those big soppy eyes. No one respected Melissa's things, and she was fed up of being the eldest, and having to be responsible.

So, refusing all offers of help, she picked up the dustpan and brush, and told Angus to STAY OUT! She would do it all over again, by herself: put everything back, hoover up the soil, and re-pot her poor pansy. But she wouldn't speak to a single soul.

Mum brought a tray up to her room after she'd missed lunch and refused dinner. Melissa wouldn't open the door, even though she was hungry. She only left her room once, to get the vacuum cleaner, some fresh soil from her dad's potting shed, and a little enamel watering can he'd given her for her last birthday, so she could rescue her flower. The pansy's little clown-like face, which usually smiled back at her, looked most unhappy.

When the glass from the broken photo frame had been carefully picked up, piece by piece, and everything else was almost spick and span again (apart from the carpet, which might need shampooing, she thought) Melissa turned her full attention to the pansy. As she worked at repotting it, she spoke soothing words to the little flower to say how sorry she was for the accident, and she found her sunnier temper almost returning.

She could hear Angus giggling as Mum gave him his bath. She really wanted to join them, but she felt silly having been so stubborn all day, and she was still upset because she had,

after all, had to do the same clean-up twice.
Her whole sunny Saturday had vanished! Her
forehead crinkled, her mouth drooped at the
edges and, as she patted down the fresh soil
around her pansy, fresh tears started to splash:
she hardly needed the watering can.

"You should never ever plant *anything* – herbs or flowers or trees – when you're grumpy and cross," said a little voice through Melissa's open window. The voice sounded musical and sweet, and somehow both grown-up and girlish. "They won't grow at all well, you know."

Melissa was startled. She looked out of the window: she was far too high up to hear anyone from the garden below, and it was too late for any of her friends to be playing outside. And anyway, the voice had sounded so near, and not quite like any of her friends.

"When you make any little garden, or even plant one single flower seed, you are talking to nature," the voice continued. Now it seemed to be coming from just above Melissa, somewhere in the branches of her tree. It was the silkiest voice she'd ever heard, full of soft laughter.

"Gardens are magical places," it went on, "and they have the power to make you feel well and happy. Special things happen in them, but first you must look after your flowers and plants with love and sunshine."

Melissa's gloomy mood lifted, and her eyes

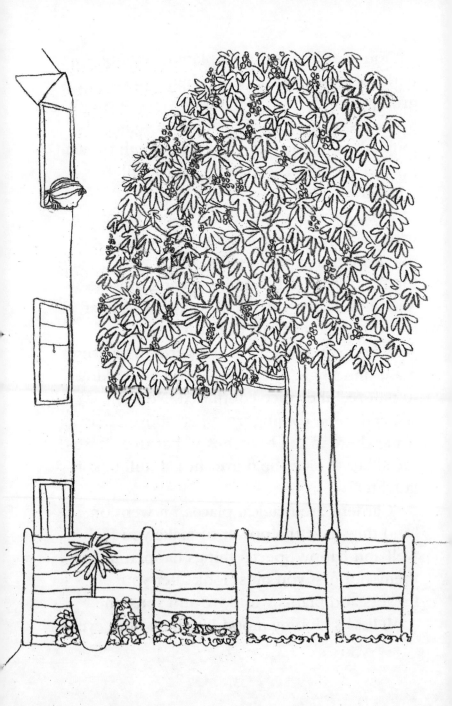

widened. She saw what seemed to be a small white flower, with a deep honey-yellow centre. She could see very clearly that it was perched on the chestnut bough above her window sill. Looking closer, she saw a tiny lady in a beautiful silk-white dress, with spiralling blonde curls floating down her back.

The dress was strapless, pulled in tight to the waist, with skirts that flowed outwards and swept down to her knees in five beautiful, yellow-edged, petal-shaped gathers.

It was like the most gorgeous ballet-dress
she'd ever seen – a little like a wedding dress.
    Melissa couldn't take her eyes away, and
she leaned against the open window to get a
better look.

Complete surprise made her forget her manners. "Who *are* you?" she asked.

The answer was gentle laughter, as sweet as a river of coconut icing. "Well, now that you're not so angry, I'll tell you! I don't think you'd have been in the right mood to hear me before."

She smiled at Melissa warmly, and did a very elegant curtsey as she spoke: "My name is Frangipani, and my sisters have nicknamed me the Sunlight Fairy because of my sunny yellow hair. But most of my friends call me Franni, and you can too, if you like!"

Melissa was absolutely astonished. She was eight years old, going on for nine; she didn't *believe* in fairies any more. She thought someone must be playing a clever trick on her, and she leaned further out of her window and looked down at the back garden to see if anyone was watching her; but there was no one out there.

"Where on earth did you come from? And, um, are you, um, *real?*"

Franni giggled, a delicious, rich sound. "What a very strange question. Can you see me, Melissa?"

She waved her arms at her and smiled, like someone trying to attract attention.

Now Melissa was quite sure she was being tested. "Yes, of course I can see you. But I don't know what you are. Are you a ..." (she had to think of the word for a second) "...a hologram? They have them at Disneyland, and in the Science Museum. They're very clever and interesting; but they're just images, and not *real* people."

"Well," said Franni, determined not to be offended, "I am certainly not one of those. I am quite as real as anybody. Not everyone can see me, it's true. But if you can talk to flowers and birds and plants and trees and cats and goldfish and rabbits, then chances are you probably will eventually be able to talk to me too. Does that help?"

Melissa grinned. It was as if the fairy had read her mind – or knew all about her. At one time or another, she had certainly talked to all of these creatures. She loved chatting with her cat and her rabbit; and to *flowers,* she thought, smiling properly.

"My Nan loves flowers and plants, and she taught me to love them too, so I suppose I do

talk to them sometimes. I love to talk to my little pansy, because she seems to listen to me so wisely. I can tell her everything – and she always keeps my secrets."

Franni suppressed a grin at this – if only Melissa knew that it was her pansy who had told the Frangipani Fairies about her troubles!

"But I'm sure I've never seen you here before," continued Melissa.

"Well, I'm often around," Franni assured her, "but I can't always talk to people. Whenever they put their feelings into a flower, though, like you have, it's easier for me. That's when I find I have lots of things that I want to say to them. And you know, you really should never take a bad temper out on your flowers.

They will thrive if you give them your sunniest thoughts and kindest heart. They won't grow at all well if you're grumpy, because they're *very* sensitive. Even when you speak too loudly, the sounds can actually *hurt* them."

Melissa felt she ought to explain to Franni *why* she was so upset, even though it seemed ridiculous to be talking to a tiny, rather grown-up looking girl on a bough of her favourite tree.

"My brother, Angus –"

Franni put up her hand to stop her. "My sisters and I heard about the whole thing from your pansy –" Melissa's eyes widened "– and I've been watching you cleaning up the mess from the branch here for a little while now. Some things are worth being upset by, Melissa; but a little brother who untidies your desk and knocks over a few books is *not* one of them!"

Melissa forgot for a moment how strange it was to be talking to someone who said she was a fairy and, realising what Franni had just said, she asked, "You have sisters? I'd *love* to have a sister. And have you really been watching me clean up?"

Franni nodded her head happily at both questions, her long curls shaking gently. "I have two sisters – though they look quite different from me. We are adopted sisters, because I left my real family a long time ago, but we're all very close. We were brought together at Kew Gardens. My home used to be in Australia, and my younger sister Plumeria – we call her "Plum" – came from California. My elder sister, Leya, comes from the Hawaiian Islands. She loves to go surfing, practically anywhere. She rides on the backs of goldfish, and even body surfs in lily ponds!"

Franni
moved nearer
to Melissa,
coming to the
very tip of the
branch which
brushed against
her bedroom
window.
Franni's skin was
fine and smooth
and, when she
tossed her curls, a
magical fragrance, a
little like jasmine flowers,
filled the air. Melissa could see
that she had very small wings just
above the top of her dress, at the back. They
weren't silvery, like her own dress-up fairy
wings; but had a dozen pearly pale colours in
them. Soft yellows, and greens, and palest
pinks were the main colours Melissa could
identify. The wings were as shiny and delicate
as soap bubbles.

Franni slid down a leaf, and landed neatly
on Melissa's window sill.

"Where do you live?" Melissa asked her.

"Not too far from here. Our house is a frangipani tree in the Palm House at Kew. Have you ever seen a tree like that, Melissa?"

Franni looked up at the little girl in inquiry, and Melissa shook her head.

"They're very pretty," Franni explained to her, "and they smell like sunshine and happy dreams. For me, living there is just like being in Sydney, because the Palm House is always warm, and the air always smells scented and earthy. We love it, and we have lots of friends there – they all originally came from other, warmer countries around the world. My younger sister, Plum, is very good at decorating, so she's made it comfortable and pretty for us. The tree was even featured in a gardening programme on television once, but I don't think anyone noticed we were there!"

The fairy spoke so brightly that it made Melissa think of sunshine after a day of rain. Franni, enjoying the look of wonder on Melissa's face, rushed on: "We've known about you for a little while. Leya was canoeing in a walnut shell in your next-door neighbour's fountain when she heard you crying one day.

She abseiled down your drainpipe to find out what was wrong. Leya's ever so good at sport." Melissa, fascinated, put out her hand without thinking, and Franni was in her palm in a second. She definitely wasn't a hologram! Melissa placed her softly on the desk, near the pansy, then noticed her palm was tickling slightly.

"So, when today's upset happened, we got a message on the fairy-phone and I came over here to see you for myself," continued Franni. "This is a job for me, you see."

Melissa could hardly take all this in. "A message? On a fairy-phone? *What's* the job for you?"

The sound of Franni's laughter floated everywhere. "We get text messages on our fairy-phone, and we print them out on large frangipani leaves. Sounds are transported from the plants and flowers that hear you – if they like you – and they arrive as words in our own fairy language to our phone. I can sort of smell what they say, even before I read them or listen to the message. Sometimes the messages come out like little songs – especially if a bird sends us part of the story."

Melissa didn't say one word. She couldn't take her eyes off Franni, as she drank in the

sounds and the beautiful scent of the fairy. She felt she was under a magic spell.

"And *I* am the right one for the job because I'm the most light-hearted of my sisters. I see something funny in everything. Nothing ever gets me down for long, so when somebody I like is in a grey mood, I can usually jolly them out of it. We each have our different strengths. My sister Plum is a wonderful cook and party girl. She's the best entertainer ever, and comes alive at night. She sings, dances, sparkles brightly and makes everyone feel fantastic.

I suppose if I'm Sunlight, she's Sunset: always in deep, velvety-red coloured dresses, like the colours of the sun in the sky on a hot summer's night. She has jet black hair, which she wears in hundreds of different styles; and she has the prettiest face. She's my bouncy little sister – full of energy even when everyone else is exhausted! She never gets nervous or worried."

Franni hardly paused. She knew Melissa's bad mood was now long gone.

"My big sister Leya is a fairy with attitude. She'll jump into anything when she needs to show someone how to find their courage. She'll sword-fight a hornet with a pine-needle, tame a growling dog, hang-glide over a playground. She's scaled the Great Yellow Sunflower in your dad's herbaceous border; and she's even helped push your nice friend Sarah up the rope in gym class! We knew about Sarah because she grows lovely sweet-peas on her patio. Do you remember when she used to be too frightened to climb high?"

Melissa rested her head in both hands, and nodded slowly. She could hardly believe what Franni was saying. She *did* remember Sarah

being frightened of climbing up the rigging, until one day she just said, "I really feel like I'll be able to do it this time! I'm going to make it!" And then, sure enough, she was higher up than anyone, in seconds. Quite a turnaround.

Franni continued. "Leya's so much braver than I am. She says everything is possible, if you believe you can do it. I can fly, but that's my limit – so I'm just here to cheer you up!"

At that moment, Franni slid down Melissa's school ruler (a lovely pink one), landing neatly upside down with her feet in the air, hair all over her face. Melissa burst out laughing, then smiled at the fairy. The inside of her dress was like yellow velvet; and there was dew on the edge, like jewelled beads.

Melissa noticed Franni's shoes: elegant white satin ballet pumps with tiny yellow bows, and ribbons criss-crossed up over her ankles. They were beautiful. Melissa suddenly felt full of joy.

Franni smiled at her, and then looked down at the bed-room floor. The little girl had done her best with the soil trodden into the carpet, but it still looked awful. Franni tilted her head to one side and considered for a moment, then she nodded a "yes", as though she had come to an important decision.

"This calls for some real fairy magic," Franni offered, pointing at the mess. "I'm going to get some of my friends in here to help."

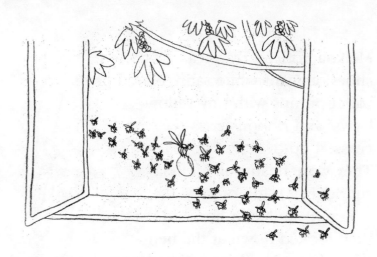

Chapter Four

Without quite knowing why, or what was happening exactly, Melissa felt a sudden change in the mood and the light in her room. She watched as Franni leant down and whispered something to the pansy's little clown-face, which seemed to make the flower smile; and then, in a moment, a swarm of bees flew in through the window. They were accompanied by a beautiful dragonfly, who was carrying something brightly-coloured and silken. Melissa thought the bees looked as if they were wearing little bow-ties, like the one Daddy wore when he went to weddings.

"What can we do about this, boys?" Franni said, floating down to the stained patch on the floor.

The bees didn't seem to answer, but Melissa found they were assembling quickly in some kind of formation, like the airforce planes she'd once seen with her dad at a flyover ceremony. This neat little squadron made two great sweeps, close to the ground, so that the soil flew up in a little cloud of earthy dust. Behind them, the dragonfly took two of the corners on one side of what he had been carrying: it appeared to be a small silk handkerchief. Franni caught hold of the two corners on the other side of the fabric, so that it resembled a colourful parachute. Together they flew along behind the cloud, collecting the soil in the silk. The whole operation took perhaps ten seconds, and the carpet was spotless when they'd finished.

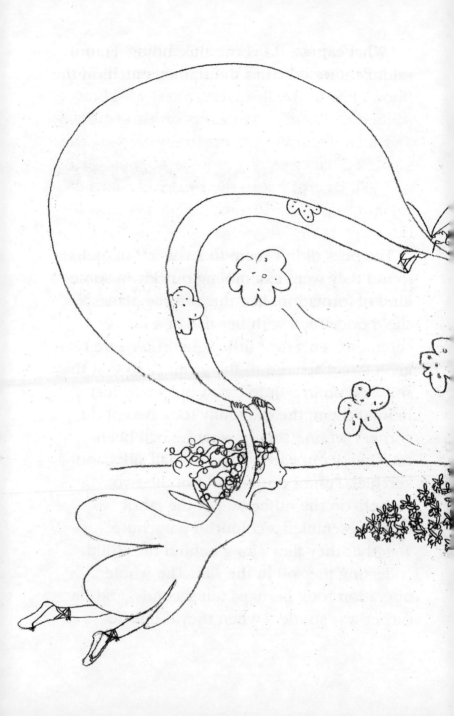

"*Much* better," said Franni, smiling enthusiastically. "Thank you, one and all." She blew a kiss to the flying creatures, who bowed politely to Franni – and afterwards to Melissa – and then departed, the dragonfly carrying the soil-filled handkerchief as he left behind them.

"He'll return that to the garden somewhere tonight," Franni explained. "Your plants will be happy to have it back."

Melissa was enchanted – even her carpet now smelled slightly of honey! "Couldn't you do our whole house like that?" she asked her tiny new friend.

"Your mother's Dyson is probably more efficient; but this is perfect when it's earth from the garden. Every little bit of it should go back to the flower beds. You can't imagine how such little things can make such a big difference to the world. Planting all these lovely seeds or not leaving your tap running while you clean your teeth has just the same effect."

Melissa was giggling and nodded sweetly to Franni, when she suddenly heard the sound of Mum's footsteps on the stairs.

"Ooh, I'd better be off," Franni said hurriedly. "There are still just a few things that grown-ups don't really understand." She winked at Melissa. "But I'll come back another time. I'll leave you my card. You can use it if you need to call me. And whenever you do, you'll find I'm very close by."

Melissa held out her hand to receive a small card-shaped item which seemed nearly as big as Franni. It had come from inside the petals of her flowery dress. It was a tiny bar of pale yellow soap, which you could see straight through. There was a beautiful flower that looked just like Franni sealed in its centre.

The bar was inlaid with the words:
FRANGIPANI FAIRIES, Inc., and it had the
name "Franni" inscribed on the bottom. It
smelled exactly like the fairy – the most
enchanting smell Melissa could remember. It
smelled so different and sweet, but somehow
familiar too. It made her think instantly of
wonderful hot summer holidays, even on a
cool May evening at home in London.

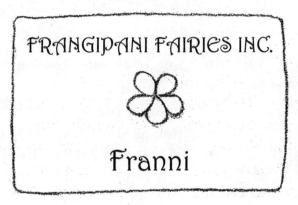

FRANGIPANI FAIRIES INC.

Franni

"Use it in your bath, or in the shower, or
just to wash your hands when you need to
cheer yourself up. Every time you talk to your
flower I can hear you, Melissa. I'll come again
soon, I promise," Franni added. "And
remember to think happy thoughts! You can
nearly always find *something* to smile about,
and it immediately makes you feel better.

Difficult moments come to us all; how you
handle them is what's important."

It was now early evening, but Franni's face
was still full of sunshine as she blew Melissa a
kiss, and then flew off in a tiny breeze just as
Melissa's mum came into the room.

Chapter Five

M elissa was still watching the window, her mouth open in silent laughter, when she heard her mother's astonished voice. The little girl noticed an equal look of amazement as her mum pushed back the door.

"My goodness! It smells fantastic in here." Her mother was surprised at how neat and clean her daughter's bedroom was again. "You must have worked very hard, Melissa. And I'm sure I heard you laughing! What was so funny?"

Melissa found that she couldn't possibly begin to explain, because she could really only just believe it herself: but her face was beaming. She threw her arms tightly around her mum. "I was thinking there's something to smile about in everything. It must have been quite funny to watch the disaster happening with Angus – I just couldn't stand back and see it then. Besides, I was *very* worried about my flower. It depends on me, you know!"

Mum looked doubtful. "That's a big change of heart, but I think it sounds very grown up, and I'm glad to hear it." She smiled at her daughter approvingly, then noticed she was holding onto something. "What's that in your hand, Melissa?" She looked carefully at the tiny bar of soap.

"It's fairy soap – guaranteed to help me find my smile when I've been silly! It has the scent of a frangipani flower. Did you know they come from Australia? And would you believe me if I told you that a little fairy gave it to me?"

Mum sniffed it, and smiled with surprise. "I don't care who gave it to you. Something's helped you recover your good mood. I can't work out exactly how, but I won't ask. You've done a wonderful job in here, Melissa – your room looks better than ever, and it smells like a flower shop. You're so lucky to have a window over the garden – the scents must always cheer you up."

"Oh yes, I love *all* the wonderful things that come through my window." Melissa was glowing, and her face looked really pretty. "And Mum, I'm *very* hungry."

Mum gave her a big squeeze. "You must be! Let's get you something to eat. There's still a tray laid for you downstairs."

Melissa took Mum's hand. Downstairs in the kitchen, she found the prettiest pink tray set with sandwiches, some strawberries, elderflower cordial, and a white-iced fairy cake Mum must have made that afternoon. And on top of the cake was a pretty white flower, with a perfumed yellow centre.

"I didn't put that there," said Mum, surprised.

"That's all right, Mum, I think I know who did." Melissa giggled, and her laughter sounded like music to her mother's ears. They looked at each other like two friends sharing a secret – although Melissa knew Mum wasn't *exactly* sure what the secret was. Some things were just impossible to explain – even to your mother.

"I'd like to wash my hands before I eat." Doing this without being reminded amazed her mother, who watched Melissa disappear into the bathroom with the cake of soap and a big grin. As she rinsed her hands and turned the tap off again tightly, Melissa realised she couldn't wait until bath-time! The world was going to be a sunnier place to live in from now on, she promised herself – especially now that she knew for a fact that there were fairies keeping a friendly eye on her.

When Melissa went up to bed an hour later,
she was exhausted from a day of unexpected
housework, but still smiling like someone who
has had a whole weekend of treats.

The first thing she did was to check that her pansy was comfortable beside her desk, back on the window sill. She stroked its petals very softly, and was delighted to see its little clown face laughing back at her happily as usual. She kissed her fore-finger and touched it to the little eye in the centre of the flower's face. Did it smile back at her? She felt sure it had, so she winked at it to say goodnight, just as Franni had winked at her earlier.

Now feeling very sleepy, she pulled her pyjamas from under the pillow of her freshly made-up bed. A familiar creamy white and yellow flower was also hiding there; and the little tub of 'Glitter Body Gel' which had caught her mother unawares that morning was completely empty.

A note was scratched onto a long, broad-shaped leaf:

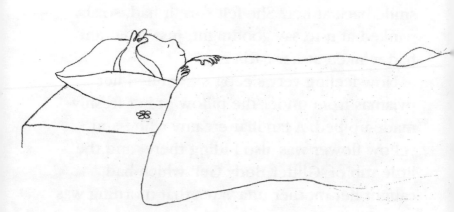

May I try this myself?
Plum the party girl will love it too. Thanks for sharing your things, Melissa. Sleep sweetly.
Franni XXX

Climbing into bed, Melissa's eyelids were already drooping. She fell asleep straight away with a gentle smile on her face, and the scent of frangipani invading her dreams. She felt like she was floating high above the river in warm sunshine.

But a mile or so away, on the branch of a magical *plumeria* tree, a party was just getting started. Enjoying the moonlight from inside their beautiful glass palace that was the Palm House at Kew – where visitors come every day without noticing anything unusual – three small figures danced in the silver light. Their tiny limbs glittered as they twirled, making it seem as though there was a lustre of sunlight even on this beautiful late evening under the moon and stars. Laughter floated out over the gardens, and soft singing could be heard – if you listened with your heart.

The End

Franni's green fairy tips:

* Plant seeds and watch them grow – but don't forget to water them!

* Everything in the garden is there for a reason – that pebble you picked up might shelter a snail, while the soil helps feed the plants – so remember to put everything back where you got it from.

* Watch the water you use in the house – every drop is precious! Be like Melissa and turn your taps off tightly.

* Remember to put your rubbish in the wastepaper basket – or, better still, recycle it!

❀ Hello dear friends ❀

This is a very important message, and it comes to you
with love from all of the fairies. I need to give you a very
special secret recipe, about how to turn a grey,
uninteresting day into a sunny, happy one.
It's a fairy spell! Are you ready?

❀

First, you need to put on your favourite coloured skirt
or pair of jeans of a happy colour. I usually choose
yellow, but Plum prefers red and Leya likes pink.
What's your choice?
Whatever you wear affects your mood.

❀

Second (and this is important), you need to find a
beautiful-smelling flower — either growing in a pot or in
your garden, or even from a bunch in a vase.
Our favourites are roses (wonderful!), frangipanis
(of course, but not everyone has one!), and violets.
I also love sweet peas, and lilac on trees in England, and
wisteria (if you have some, like Melissa) is just magical.

❀

Third, you need to close your eyes and really smell the
flower. Is it sweet? Strong? Gentle? Light? Breathe in and
imagine all the beautiful things you can. Inside your head,
say one nice thing to someone you like. Then, make a

simple wish for something sunny and special to happen to them, and also to you. Don't think too much about what it is, though. Fairies like to work in surprises!
And when you open your eyes (here's the most important part of the wish-spell) you need to really smile at the flower, and at the world.

❀

Okay — that's it! Simple! Now you have a good day, and look for another story from us soon. What lovely things will happen to you today? Have you wished strongly enough? Oh, and by the way, a spell ALWAYS works best if you do something nice for someone else, straight afterwards. Can you help your dad in the garden? Or your mum with some baking? Could you plant a few flowers for me to see growing soon?

Good luck, everyone!

❀ Love, Franni xxx ❀

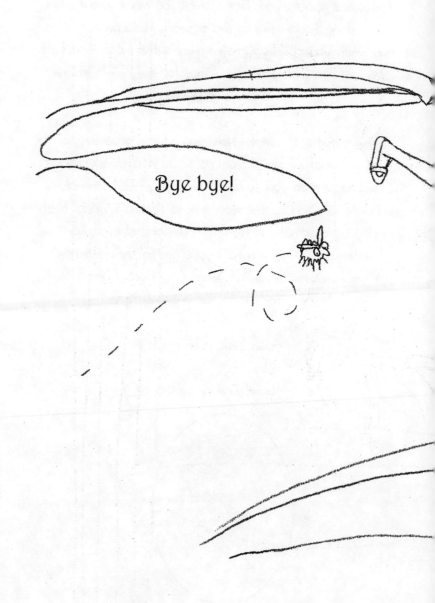

Bye bye!

IF YOU ENJOYED THE SUNLIGHT FAIRY,
LOOK OUT FOR THE FRANGIPANI FAIRIES'
NEXT ADVENTURE, IN

THE SUNRISE FAIRY –

HERE'S A TASTER OF WHAT'S IN STORE!

On the summery day that she first met Araminta, Franni the Frangipani Fairy had been sightseeing inside the great building of Westminster Abbey, along with hundreds of other tourists.

Franni loved learning about history, so she took any opportunity to float out of the heat and into the cool of the church, where she flew from one flower arrangement to the next, completely unnoticed. Her dress made her look just like a little yellow flower blossom floating along on the breeze and none of the bustling tourists gave her a second glance as they looked at the wonderful brass statues, and the tombs of past kings and queens.

But on this particular day in June it had been so stuffy in the busy abbey that Franni had gone outside to get some fresh air. She had flown down to the river and jumped on a busy ferry-boat, which had taken her away from the beautiful outline of the Houses of Parliament and Big Ben, a mile or so up-river. And it was here, in one of the flats around a garden square set back from the river-bank, that she had heard Araminta laughing. Laughter is a sound that *always* reaches fairies' ears - and on this particular day it made Franni happy and very curious.

Araminta – whose family called her 'Minty' – was helping her dad in the garden. The space looked rather bare and needed a lot of work, with digging and planting, but Minty was delighted to help out. She had proper gardening gloves and tools, and some little seed packets and potted flowers around her. When the work was too rough, or there was nothing else she could do, she brought fresh drinks from inside the house to cool them both down. She and her father worked well together and spent hours outside in the heat, but Minty's elder sister Bella wasn't even a tiny bit interested in the new garden. She thought the work was too 'dirty' for her neatly painted nails!

When Minty's mum brought some sandwiches out for the pair of gardeners at lunch-time, Minty carried her plate down to the bottom of the garden to sit in the shade of the apple tree. Looking up into the cool branches, she saw a beautiful flower of a distinctly different colour and shape from the white apple blossom, which was nearly finished.

She realised at once that she was looking at something special, and she smiled, before asking Franni very politely, "Excuse me, but are you a fairy? I really think you must be."

Minty was not at all rude, and perhaps only slightly surprised to see her guest.

"You're very perceptive, Minty! How do you do? I'm Franni, a Frangipani Fairy, and it's a pleasure to meet you. What a lot you've done in the garden! I don't recall there ever being anything pretty growing here before."

Then Franni jumped very lightly down from the branch and landed elegantly on the wooden bench where Minty was sitting with her sandwich.

Franni learned that Minty's family had only recently bought the flat. Her father wanted to make the garden a pretty place to be in as quickly as possible, so they could all enjoy it for the summer; and his younger daughter seemed only too happy to help out. She spent hours in the garden working and watering, chattering to birds and bees and beetles and flowers, and she especially adored the butter-flies who now found a home in the flowering buddleia bushes.

Minty wondered thoughtfully where all of these beautiful creatures must have played before her father had planted flowers and trees for them.

By the end of the summer the garden looked colourful and tidy, and Minty was perfectly settled and at peace in her new home. She was not missing her old friends nearly as much as she had expected. But the one thing that was worrying her was starting her new school. She was comfortable with plants and animals and one or two close friends, but she didn't find it easy fitting in with crowds and strangers.

As the first day of the school year got closer, Minty became more and more concerned. She confided to the plants she tended to so lovingly that she was really quite shy!

Her elder sister, Bella, had already had a week at the new school when they first moved down to London at the end of the previous school year; but Minty had had a bad cold at the time and her mum had decided to keep her at home rather than sending her to a new, strange place when she was feeling so ill. So now Minty had to start her new school year without having met anyone over the holidays – and she knew Bella would think it wasn't 'cool' to talk to her little sister at break, or even on the bus. It made Minty feel very nervous.

The three fairy sisters thought about this problem as they had tea together one afternoon with the butterflies in Minty's lovely garden. It wasn't long before Leya had a simple idea: "Why don't I go along with her – at least for the first day? Then I can keep an eye on her from a distance."

"That's a wonderful idea, Leya," Franni agreed. "No one else has to know you're there; but if the day gets boring, you're sure to find a way to liven things up! Don't you think so, Plum?"

The youngest, ruby-dressed fairy giggled and nodded, along with her brightly-coloured butterfly companions.

And so it was that at seven o'clock on a Tuesday morning in early September, Leya the Frangipani Fairy was preparing for her own very first day at school ...

Franni, Leya and Plum are the Frangipani Fairies. Their playmates are animals and insects; their home a giant frangipani tree . . .

Elder sister Leya is full of energy and excitement, so when she hears that Minty's miserable about going to a new school, she decides to get the little girl's first day off to a great start – with the help of the class goldfish and a beautiful butterfly!

ISBN 1416910840
EAN 9781416910848

Frangipani Fairies

'Fairy Power' Website

If you liked this story you'll love the Frangipani Fairies website!

Log on to www.frangipanifairies.com to join in the fun and become a member of the Petal Power Club!

❀ Meet each of the fairies and find out more about their special powers

❀ Join the Petal Power Club and help save the world around us!

❀ Read the fairy BLOG, find green tips and download icons

❀ Plus extracts from the books and fairy land quizzes

It's fun being a fairy!